Woodbridge Town Library
Woodbridge, CT 06525

A2180 183138 7

W9-BRK-707

61/07

E DUE

THREE LITTLE CAJUN PIGS

by Mike Artell

illustrated by Jim Harris

Dial Books for Young Readers

For dem folks south of I-10 who know how to pass a good time. —MA

To my little brother, Paul, and his Special Olympics basketball team from Shepherd's Home. —JH

DIAL BOOKS FOR YOUNG READERS
A division of Penguin Young Readers Group
Published by The Penguin Group
Penguin Group (USA) Inc., 375 Hudson Street, New York, NY 10014, U.S.A.
Penguin Group (Canada), 90 Eglinton Avenue East, Suite 700, Toronto, Ontario, Canada M4P 2Y3 (a division of Pearson Penguin Canada Inc.)
Penguin Books Ltd, 80 Strand, London WC2R 0RL, England
Penguin Ireland, 25 St. Stephen's Green, Dublin 2, Ireland (a division of Penguin Books Ltd)
Penguin Group (Australia), 250 Camberwell Road, Camberwell, Victoria 3124, Australia (a division of Pearson Australia Group Pty Ltd)
Penguin Books India Pvt Ltd, 11 Community Centre, Panchsheel Park, New Delhi - 110 017, India
Penguin Group (NZ), Cnr Airborne and Rosedale Roads, Albany, Auckland 1310, New Zealand (a division of Pearson New Zealand Ltd)
Penguin Books (South Africa) (Pty) Ltd, 24 Sturdee Avenue, Rosebank, Johannesburg 2196, South Africa
Penguin Books Ltd, Registered Offices: 80 Strand, London WC2R 0RL, England

Text copyright © 2006 by Mike Artell • Illustrations copyright © 2006 by Jim Harris
All rights reserved
The publisher does not have any control over and does not assume
any responsibility for author or third-party websites or their content.
Designed by Lily Malcom • Text set in Granjon
Manufactured in China on acid-free paper
10 9 8 7 6 5 4 3 2 1

Library of Congress Cataloging-in-Publication Data
Artell, Mike.
 Three little Cajun pigs / by Mike Artell ; illustrated by Jim Harris.
   p. cm.
Summary: In this rhyming version of the familiar folktale, a big bad gator comes after
the three pig brothers, Ulysse, Thibodeaux, and Trosclair, in the Louisiana bayou.
 ISBN 0-8037-2815-8
[1. Pigs—Folklore. 2. Folklore.] I. Harris, Jim, date, ill. II. Title.
 PZ8.1.A77 Th 2006
 398.24'529633—dc21
                      2002004705

The full-color artwork was prepared using watercolor
and pencil on Strathmore rag bristol.

GLOSSARY

BAYOU—pronounced "BAH-you," it is a small stream.

CHER—pronounced "share" (the R is very soft), it is a term of affection meaning "dear."

COUCHON DE LAIT—pronounced "COO-shawn de LAY." These words mean "milk-fed pig." At many festivals in Louisiana, Cajuns roast a pig to eat.

DERRIERE—pronounced "dairy-AIR," it is French for "behind."

MON AMI—pronounced "mawn ah-ME," it is French for "my friend."

MON FRER—pronounced "mawn FRAIR," it is French for "my brother."

ROUX—pronounced "roo," it is a mixture of oil and flour that is stirred over heat until it is brown. Other ingredients are added to a roux to make Cajun dishes such as gumbo. Many Cajun recipes start with the words "First, make a roux."

THIBODEAUX—pronounced "TIB-boe-doe," it is also a common Cajun name.

TOUT DE SUITE—pronounced "toot SWEET," it is French for "quickly."

TROSCLAIR—can be pronounced "TROSS-clair" or "tross-CLAIR." It is a common Cajun name.

ULYSSE—pronounced "you-LEASE," it is a Cajun first name.

Note: The rhyming scheme for *Three Little Cajun Pigs* emphasizes the second, fifth, eighth, and eleventh syllables. Example:

In SOUTH Loo-si-AN-a, where GA-tors grow BIG
Live T'REE Cajun PIGS and an OL' mama PIG.

In south Loo-siana, where gators grow big,
Live t'ree Cajun pigs and an ol' mama pig.
Dem pigs was named Trosclair, and Thibodeaux too,
Ulysse was de oldest, dey all called him "Boo."

One mornin' dere mama done give 'em some food
And tell 'em some news dat don' make 'em feel good.
"It's time dat you boys find you own place to stay;
I t'ink dat you better start lookin' today.

"Go build you a house of you own," Mama say.
"You'll sleep dere tonight if you start right away."
So t'ree little pigs pack up all of dere clothes,
Kiss Mama good-bye and den follow dere nose.

Dey walk for a while, and den Trosclair he say,
"I'll build me a house, and I'll do it today.
I'll build it so fast jus' like you never saw,
I'd do it right now if I had me some straw."

Den jus' up de road by de bayou dey see,
A big wooden sign dat been nailed to a tree.
Dem pigs read de words on de sign and dey say,
"Look here! Dis straw's free! You can take it away!"

"Go on," Trosclair say, "I will catch up to you.
I'll build a straw house before you count to two."
Ol' Boo roll his eyes and he make dem big sigh,
And Thibodeaux say, "You look angry, Boo. Why?"

"Straw is okay if you making dem bed,
  But when you build walls, you need somethin' instead.
  Houses for pigs got to be plenty strong
  In case dat dem gator come crawlin' along."

Den jus' up de road, guess what bot' dem pigs see . . .
Somebody been cuttin' some limbs off a tree.
And dere was a sign dat say, "Haul dese away."
And Thibodeaux shout, "Dis is my lucky day!"

He grab all dem limbs and start workin' so fas',
His house halfway finished 'fore too much time pass.
Ulysse, he start t'inkin', "Dem boys got it wrong;
If you build a house, den it's got to be strong."

Ulysse shake his head and den he walk some more
And soon dat pig see just what he's lookin' for.
A whole bunch o' bricks was piled next to a sign
Dat say, "Need dese bricks? You can have 'em, dat's fine."

Boo clear off a spot for his house made of brick.
He build dat house strong, and he make dem walls thick.
An' while he was workin', who come skippin' by?
Dem two udder pigs, and dey laugh 'til dey cry.

"Dem bricks sho' look heavy. What's wrong wit' you, Boo?
How come you don't use straw or sticks like we do?"
Boo frown and he say, "When dat gator come by,
he'll knock your house down wit' his tail if he try."

An' speakin' of gators, not too far away,
Somebody was watchin' dem little pigs play.
Ol' Claude, dat big gator, was in de bayou,
He see dem t'ree pigs and he watch what dey do.

Claude crawl out de water and hide in de grass,
And sit dere and wait 'til dem first two pigs pass.
Den Claude jump in front of dem pigs and he say,
"I t'ink dat it's time for some couchon de lait!"

Ol' Claude start to chase de first pig dat he saw . . .
Trosclair, he's de one wit' de house made of straw.
Trosclair he run home and den shut dat door tight,
He pull close dem curtains and turn off de light.

"Oh piggy," say Claude with dat big gator smile,
"Could I come inside of you house for a while?"
 Dat's when Trosclair shout, "*No!* I won't let you in;
 Not by all dem hairs dat I got on my chin."

"Hmm . . ." growl Ol' Claude in dat deep gator voice.
"Now piggy, you lef' me wit' no udder choice."
 Ol' Claude hiss and puff and he make his face frown,
 He wiggle a little and turn hisself roun'.

And WHACK! when dat gator done flip his tail hard,
Dat straw house go flyin' all over de yard.
Trosclair look at Claude and he cry, "You so big,
You jus' a mean bully. Why pick on us pig?"

"Ha ha," Ol' Claude laugh. "Mon ami, don' get mad,
Between you and me . . . dat straw house was some bad."
Den Trosclair he turn and as quick as a mouse,
He run to where Thibodeaux build de stick house.

When Thibodeaux see Ol' Claude chasin' Trosclair,
He say, "Hurry up, you'll be safe here, mon frer!"
Dey run in dat stick house and lock all de door,
Den peek out to see if Claude comin' some more.

"Oh piggies," say Claude with dat big gator smile,
"Could I come inside of you house for a while?"
Dem little pigs shout, "*No!* We won't let you in;
Not by all dem hairs dat we got on our chin."

"Okay," say Ol' Claude, "you can have it your way,
But I don't like workin' dis hard every day."
Ol' Claude hiss and puff and he make his face frown,
He wiggle a little and turn hisself roun'.

And WHACK! when dat gator done flip his tail hard,
Dat stick house go flyin' all over de yard.
Dat's all dem pigs needed to scare 'em to death,
Dey jump up and run 'til dey plumb outta breath.

Now, inside his house, Boo was busy fo' true
He had a big pot and was makin' a roux.
He stir dat roux good 'cause Ulysse he done learn
You gotta keep stirrin' or roux's gonna burn.

Den out in de yard Ulysse hear all dat noise,
He t'ink to himself, "*Now* what's wrong wit' dem boys?"
He open de door but befo' he could fuss,
Dem udder pigs cry, "Boo! Ol' Claude's after us!"

Ulysse slam de door and he turn de big lock,
And jus' when he did dat, he heard a soft knock.
"Oh piggies," say Claude with dat big gator smile,
"Could I come inside of you house for a while?"

Dem little pigs shout, "*No!* We won't let you in;
Not by all dem hairs dat we got on our chin."
So WHACK! dat ol' gator done flip his tail hard,
But dis time de house don' fall down in de yard.

Ag'in and ag'in, Claude done hit it some more,
Den he gotta stop 'cause his tail gettin' sore.
"I see dere's a chimney. Dat's how I'll get in,
And den I'll get *all* of dem hairs on your chin."

Trosclair start to whine, "What are we gonna do?
And Thibodeaux cry, "He will eat us fo' true!"
Boo shout at his brudders, "Get up off your seat!
An' bring me some wood. We gone turn up de heat."

Outside dey hear Claude on dat roof scratchin' roun'.
He don't climb so good and he keep fallin' down.
But finally he climb all de way to de top,
He jump in de chimney, den let go and drop.

Now, Claude he don' know 'bout dat roux in de pot,
But as he was fallin', he start gettin' hot.
Ol' Claude can't slow down, and he t'ink, "Dis ain't good.
If I could get out of dis chimney, I would."

But it was too late, Claude's big tail hit de roux,
And ya'll when it did, Claude don't know what to do.
"Aïeee!" shout Ol' Claude. "Someone help me tout de suite.
"My tail's burnin' up, won't you please stop de heat?"

Dem t'ree little pigs know what Claude tried to do,
But dey figure he learned his lesson fo' true.
Ulysse run and grab a big lid for dat pot,
Den put it on top so it won't be so hot.

Claude's tail came out first and de pigs had to laugh
'Cause dat gator was toasted on his bottom half.
He walked out de door kinda funny and slow,
He head down de road and de pigs watch him go.

"Ya'll have a nice day," Trosclair call wit' a smile,
Den Thibodeaux laugh, "Don' come back for a while."
But big brother Boo got his arms folded tight.
He ask, "Where y'all plannin' on sleepin' tonight?"

Dem two udder pigs dey start scratchin' dere heads
Dey ain't got no house and dey ain't got no beds.
Ulysse tell dem pigs, "Y'all can stay here tonight,
But we got to go and build bot' your house right."

De very next day, Thibodeaux and Trosclair
Done build de best houses you seen anywhere.
Ulysse show dem how dey can build dat house strong
In case dat ol' gator should come back along.

And speakin' of gators, way down de bayou
A gator we know sure was hurtin' fo' true.
He got him an ice pack on his derriere
And where dem pigs live, he ain't goin' back dere.

Now, some of dis story is true and some's not,
And which part is which, y'all . . . I guess I forgot.
But take my advice 'cause I know dat it's true:
When gators come roun', cher . . . just make you a roux.